WHO SAID RED?

WHO SAID RED?
Mary Serfozo
illustrated by Keiko Narahashi

Margaret K. McElderry Books
New York

To Dana, Sara, Jonathan, and Aaron
M.S.

For Peter and Micah
K.N.

Text copyright © 1988 by Mary Serfozo
Illustrations copyright © 1988 by Keiko Narahashi

Margaret K. McElderry Books
Macmillan Publishing Company
866 Third Avenue
New York, New York 10022
Collier Macmillan Canada, Inc.

First Edition

10 9 8 7 6 5 4 3 2 1

Composition by Linoprint Composition, New York, New York
Printed and bound by Toppan Printing Company in Japan

Library of Congress Cataloging-in-Publication Data

Serfozo, Mary.
  Who said red?

  Summary: A dialogue between two speakers, one of
whom must keep insisting on an interest in the color
red, introduces that hue as well as green, blue,
yellow, and others.
  [1. Color—Fiction]   I. Narahashi, Keiko, ill.
II. Title.
PZ7.S482Wh 1988   [E] 88-9345
ISBN 0-689-50455-1

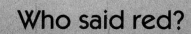
Who said red?

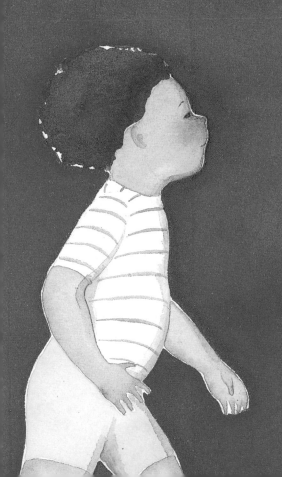

Did you say red?
A Santa red,
A stop sign red,

A cherry, berry, very red.

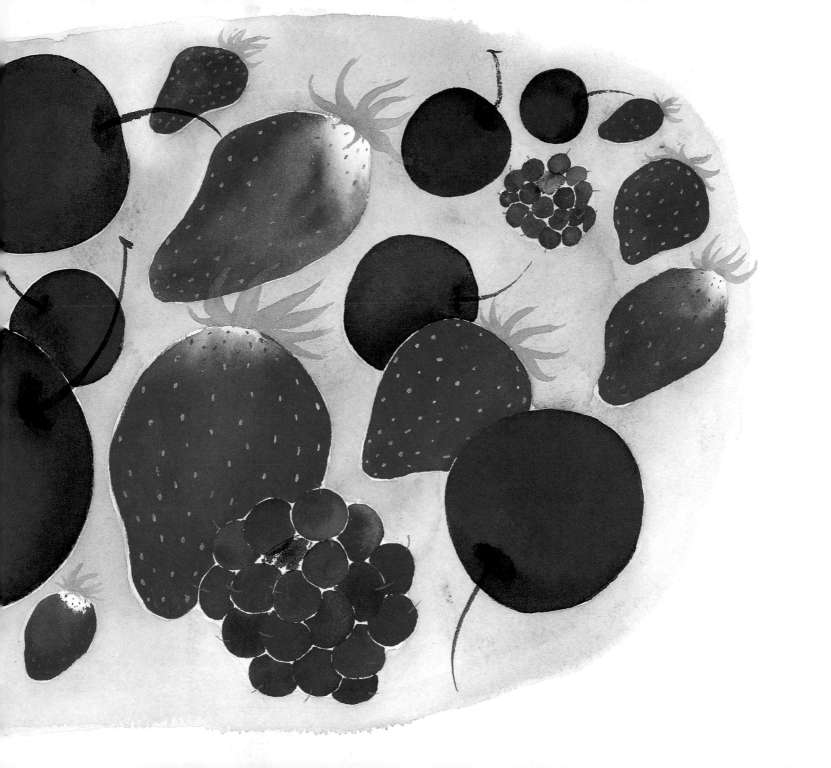

You don't mean green?
Look, here is green....

A pickle green,
A big frog green,

A leaf, a tree,
a green bean green.

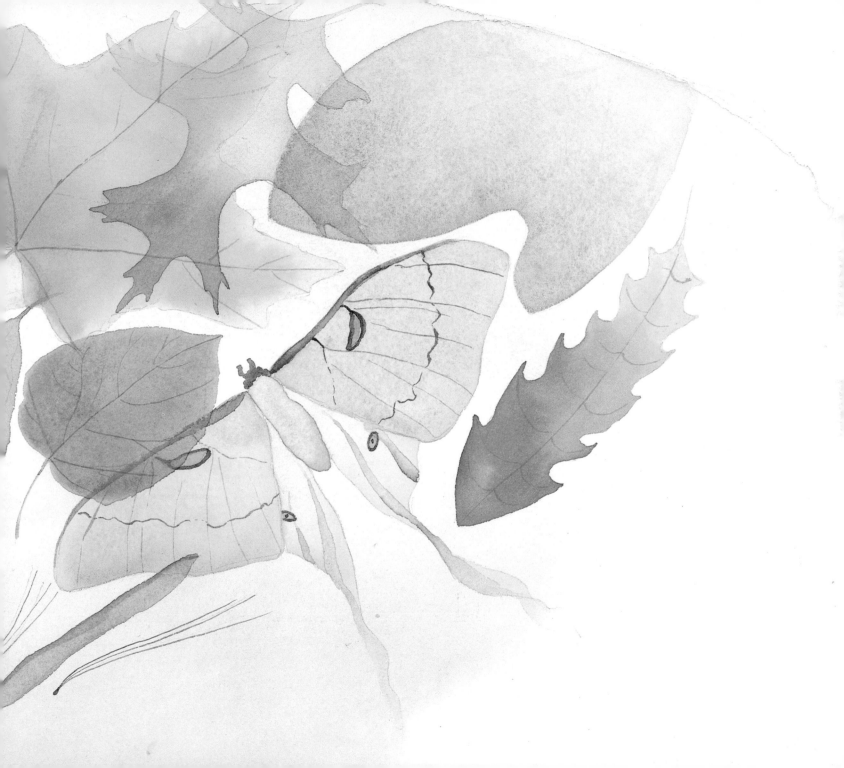

Now who said blue?
Could it be you?

A blue sky blue,
A blue eye blue,

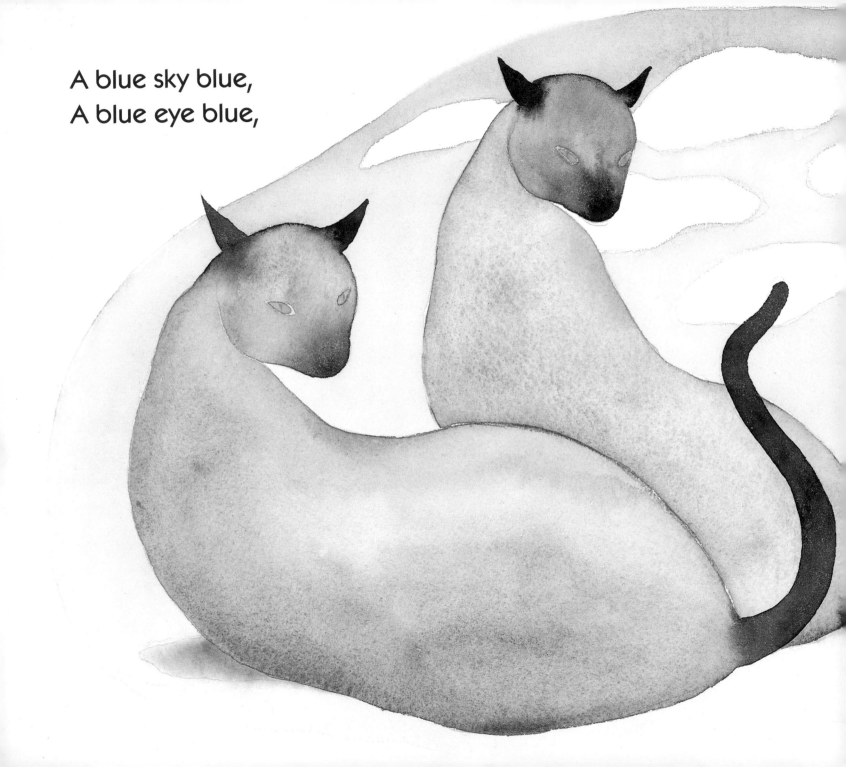

A bow, a ball, a blue jean blue.

Well hello, yellow....
Bright and mellow.

Slicker yellow,
Sunshine yellow,

Lemonade and daisy yellow.

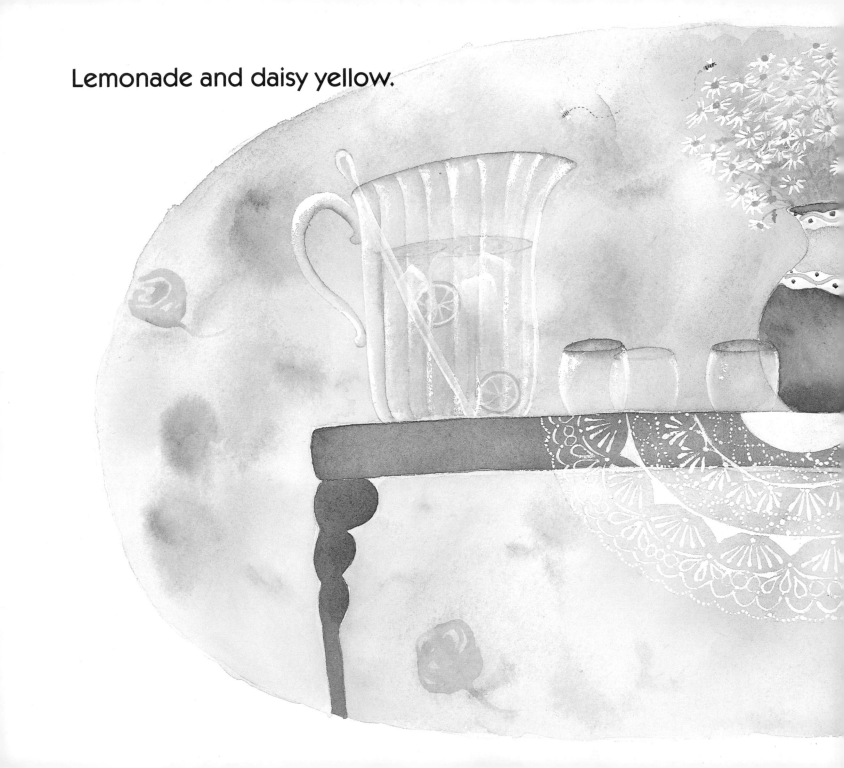

Not purple, then,
Or brown or pink…

Not orange, or black
Or white, I think.

Tell me, again,
Just what you said.

Did you say red?

YES, I SAID RED!